SCHOOL OF MISFITS

Laura Shenton

SCHOOL OF MISFITS

Laura Shenton

Iridescent Toad Publishing

Iridescent Toad Publishing.

Cover by JESSART

First edition. ISBN 978-1-8380186-7-2

Chapter One

Thick fog swallowed the boat as it cut through the deep, still waters. The sound of the oars dipping into the black surface barely rose above the quiet murmurs and nervous breathing of the two dozen students on board. Nicola sat on the boat's edge, pulling her cloak tighter around her tall, lean frame. She watched her reflection in the water – pale skin made paler by anxiety, dark silver hair falling in waves past her shoulders, green eyes that seemed to catch what little light remained in the endless night. The chill of the mist crept into her bones as she looked up. She stared ahead, trying to make out the shape of Darkmore Academy, her new prison.

Around her, other students – all in their early twenties like her – sat hunched and withdrawn, lost in their own thoughts. Some clutched bags or books to their chests; others simply stared into the fog. They were all misfits, Nicola knew, though she couldn't help but wonder what powers or secrets had brought them here. She ran her fingers over the simple silver pendant at her throat, a nervous habit she'd developed years ago.

The academy loomed somewhere in the fog, but all she could see was the void that stretched before them. It wasn't just the physical distance that made her feel so far away from everything familiar. The journey here had been demanding – both in miles and in spirit. She had once hoped to find her place in the magical world, but every school, every institution, had cast her out, fearing her power. She had grown used to the whispers, the distrust, the sideways glances. They had called her dangerous. Unstable. Even a threat.

She just didn't belong anywhere. Not with them, and not here.

The boatman, silent and hunched in his seat, gave no indication they were nearing the shore, but Nicola could feel the weight of the academy's presence pressing down on her. It was as though the very air had changed, thickened with something ancient and unseen.

Her fingers twitched involuntarily, and a flicker of shadow danced across her palm before she quickly suppressed it. The shadows responded to her emotions, and in this place, where everything felt so dark and foreboding, they were eager to escape her control. She clenched her fists, forcing the magic back down.

"There it is," the boatman said croakily, breaking the silence.

Through the fog, a shape finally emerged – tall spires and crumbling towers jutting into the night sky, barely visible in the gloom. The academy was a fortress, more like an ancient castle than a school. Its stone walls were covered in ivy, and its windows glowed faintly with the dim light of torches burning within. It looked abandoned, like a relic from a time long past. This place was still alive, though it felt like it was on its last breath.

The boat scraped against the rocky shore, and without a word, the boatman nodded for the group to disembark. One by one, everyone climbed onto land, their shoes crunching against the wet gravel. Nicola hesitated only for a moment before stepping onto the damp, uneven stones. As soon as her feet touched the ground, she felt a shiver run up her spine. Something about this place was wrong. Or maybe it was exactly right for someone like her.

"Welcome to Darkmore Academy," the boatman muttered, disinterested and gravelly.

Without waiting for a reply, he pushed away from the shore, pressing his oars against the water. Slowly, the boat began to drift away to be swallowed by the thickening fog. His form blurred, becoming a faint silhouette as he disappeared into the bleak expanse. Even the ripples in the water vanished, as though the boat had never been there at all.

The group began to split up, everyone making their way towards the academy in twos and threes, their shadows stretching long behind them in the dim light.

Nicola stood alone for a moment, staring up

at the foreboding structure. It seemed to watch her as much as she was watching it. The air was imbued with the scent of damp earth and something else – something old and musty, like decay hidden beneath the surface.

"First time here?"

The voice startled her. She spun around to see a young woman about her age standing a few feet away, leaning casually against a crooked lamp post. She had skin so pale it seemed almost translucent in the foggy light, offsetting features that might have been delicate if not for the sharp, knowing look in her eyes. Long, pitch-black hair fell in wild tangles down her back, adorned with small braids threaded with silver beads that caught the minimal light. A jagged scar ran along her left jawline, disappearing beneath her collar. Her eyes glinted with an unusual amber hue, and there was a slight smile playing on her lips, as if she knew something that no one else did.

"Yeah," Nicola replied cautiously. "You?"

"Second year," the young woman said calmly

as she pushed off from the lamp post and walked closer towards Nicola, eyeing her curiously. "You don't look like the others."

"What's that supposed to mean?"

"Most people who come here are, well… wrecks," the young woman said with a grin that didn't quite reach her eyes. "You look like you've still got some fight left in you."

"What's your name?" Nicola asked her, too uncomfortable to ask her what she meant.

"I'm Remy," she said as she extended a hand. "You?"

Nicola held back for a moment, feeling the unease stirring in her chest. She had to force herself to take the offered hand.

"I'm Nicola."

Before she could say more, a chill swept over her. The dim light from the academy's windows flickered as if something had passed in front of them. Remy's grin widened, but there was something unsettling about the way she seemed so at ease with the coldness that had surrounded them.

"You'll fit in fine," Remy said, her voice lowering to a conspiratorial whisper. "Especially with those."

Nicola followed Remy's gaze and realised with a self-conscious jolt that the shadows were curling out from beneath her sleeves, like tendrils of smoke escaping from a dying fire. Nicola quickly yanked her hands back, shoving them deep into her pockets. Remy's smirk didn't waver – she was clearly unfazed by the dark presence.

"I know a thing or two about the kind of magic that people don't want to talk about," Remy said. "You don't have to hide it here. At least, not from me."

The way Remy spoke gave Nicola pause. There was an edge to her words, something dark and dangerous that lay just beneath the surface. Despite Nicola's better judgment, she felt a flicker of relief. Maybe here, in this forsaken place, she wouldn't have to keep pretending that everything was fine.

Together, they made their way up the

crumbling stone path towards the academy's large iron gates. The fog seemed to cling to them, refusing to let go.

"Ready to see your new home?" Remy asked, her voice dripping with mock excitement.

Nicola wasn't sure this place could ever be called home. But what choice did she have?

Chapter Two

The iron gates groaned shut with a finality that sent a ripple of unease through Nicola. As she and Remy walked further towards the academy building, she looked around at her fellow arrivals dispersing slowly across the grounds, their dark clothing billowing in the low breeze. The atmosphere seemed colder inside the academy's grounds, as though the fog had seeped into the very stones of the place, draining it of warmth. The courtyard was sprawling, overgrown with tangled vines and patches of grass that had long gone wild. Statues, half crumbled and worn down by time, lined the path towards the main building, their features obscured by the creeping shadows of the night.

As she walked, the shadows around Nicola seemed to stir again, whispering at the edges of her mind. They were more restless here, as if something in the academy's grounds was calling to them. She clenched her fists, feeling the familiar tension building inside her. It had always been like this – the shadows were never fully under her control, and in places of strong magic, they were always harder to suppress.

She stole a glance at Remy, who was now leading the way with an almost casual stride. Remy seemed unnervingly comfortable in the midst of all this decay. She walked with a confidence that suggested she wasn't just used to the eerie atmosphere – she revelled in it.

The path wound through the courtyard, leading them towards the academy's large front doors. As they neared them, the torches on either side flickered, casting long, distorted shadows across the walls. For a moment, Nicola could have sworn she saw movement in the darkness – something slipping between the shadows, too quick and too fluid to be human.

"See them?" Remy asked.

"See what?" Nicola asked, stopping uncomfortably in her tracks.

"The ghosts," Remy said, turning to face Nicola with a satisfied grin. "They're always watching. They like to keep a keen eye on the new students."

"Ghosts?!"

"Yes," Remy answered, her grin widening. "This place is full of them. You'll get used to it. Some are harmless, just echoes of the past, but others... well, they're a bit more curious."

Nicola scanned the shadows. She had always felt a connection to darkness, but this was different. The shadows here were alive, filled with eyes she couldn't see but could feel on her skin. It was as if the academy itself was watching her, waiting for her to make a mistake.

"Don't worry," Remy said with a light laugh, seeming to sense Nicola's discomfort. "They won't hurt you. Not unless you give them a reason to."

"That's not reassuring."

"It's not supposed to be," said Remy, winking before pushing against the heavy wooden doors of the academy.

The doors creaked open to reveal a vast entrance hall bathed in dim, flickering light. The ceiling stretched high above them, supported by towering stone pillars carved with strange runes that pulsed faintly with magic. Dust hung in the air, caught in the faint beams of muted moonlight filtering in through the stained glass windows. The place smelt of old books, damp stone, and something metallic, like rust or dried blood.

Students moved through the hall in small groups, their hushed voices carrying a nervous energy. Some glanced at Nicola with disinterest, while others seemed to avoid her entirely, as if sensing the instability of her magic.

"Come on," Remy urged, leading Nicola towards a specific corridor. "You'll want to meet your advisor before curfew."

"Advisor?"

"Yes. The academy assigns one to every

student. It's their job to keep you from summoning something you can't control."

Remy's tone was half-joking, but the way her eyes gleamed in the low light suggested there was truth to the warning.

They walked down a narrow corridor lined with portraits of old, grim-faced academics – scholars from centuries past who had left their mark on the academy's history. Their eyes seemed to follow Nicola as she passed. The wooden floor beneath her feet creaked with each step, and the shadows felt as though they were pressing in closer, growing thicker as she ventured deeper into the academy. Every now and then, she caught a flicker of movement at the edge of her vision – a shape darting just out of sight. She couldn't tell if it was the shadows playing tricks on her, or the presence of the ghosts Remy had mentioned.

"I don't think I've asked yet," Remy said casually as they walked. "What's your deal? Why'd they send you here?"

Nicola hesitated, unsure of how much to reveal.

"I... I don't fit in anywhere else," she said eventually. "My magic... it's not like everyone else's."

"That's kind of the point of this place, isn't it?" Remy said with a laugh. "Everyone here's a little broken, a little wrong. You're in good company."

Nicola knew her magic wasn't just 'a little wrong'. It was dangerous. Unpredictable. And it wasn't something she liked talking about, not with someone she'd just met. The shadows had always been a part of her, lurking in the corners of her mind, waiting to slip free in a moment of weakness. Most people didn't understand that kind of power. Most people were afraid of it. Afraid of her.

Remy, however, seemed unfazed. If anything, she looked intrigued.

"Don't worry," Remy said, her voice lowering slightly as they neared the end of the corridor. "This place has seen worse. Whatever you've got going on, you'll fit right in here."

Nicola wasn't so sure.

At the end of the hallway, a large wooden door stood slightly ajar, warm light spilling out from within. Remy knocked twice before pushing the door open without waiting for a response.

"Professor Blackthorn's office," she informed Nicola as they stepped inside.

The room was cluttered with books, scrolls, and strange magical artefacts, many of which glowed faintly or hummed with unseen power. The air was thick with the scent of herbs and incense. Behind a large desk covered in papers sat a striking woman who commanded attention despite her slight frame. Her face was angular, with high cheekbones and obsidian eyes that seemed to hold centuries of secrets. Though she appeared to be in her late forties, her hair was silver, falling in a sleek curtain to her waist. A single streak of jet black remained, running from her temple. Her robes were a midnight blue silk that seemed to absorb the light around them, and a pendant of black opal hung at her throat, occasionally flickering with inner fire.

"Ah, a new arrival," she said, her voice smooth

but unwelcoming as she addressed Nicola. "You're late."

Nicola opened her mouth to respond, but Remy cut in:

"The boat was delayed. You know how it is with the fog."

Professor Blackthorn didn't smile. Instead, she gestured to an empty chair in front of her desk.

"Sit."

Nicola did as instructed, feeling a sense of unease settle over her as the professor continued to watch her with those piercing eyes.

"You're at Darkmore Academy because you've been cast out from other places," Professor Blackthorn said, not bothering with introductions. "Your power is unstable, dangerous, and has no place in traditional schools of magic."

The words stung, but Nicola remained silent.

"This academy is different. We take in those who do not fit elsewhere. But make no mistake – there are rules here. And if you cannot follow them, you will not survive very long."

Nicola's fingers twitched. She could feel the shadows stirring again, threatening to spill over. She had to force them down, working hard to keep her expression neutral.

Professor Blackthorn's eyes flickered to Nicola's hands, and for a brief moment, a look of concern crossed her features.

"You'll need to learn control," she said bluntly.

"I know," Nicola replied, trying to keep her voice steady, not wishing to appear confrontational.

"Good," Professor Blackthorn said, leaning back in her chair. "Because that which lives in the darkness of this place will not be as forgiving as I am."

24

Chapter Three

Professor Blackthorn's warning hung in the air long after they'd left the cluttered office. Remy didn't speak right away, and neither did Nicola. The hallway outside felt as though the very walls were pressing in on her, as though they were alive, listening, waiting.

"Don't let her get to you," Remy finally said. "She's always like that. All doom and gloom. It's probably why they match her up with first year students who've been rejected from other places."

"She's right though," Nicola said pensively. "If I don't get control over my magic..."

"You will," Remy interrupted, waving a hand dismissively. "Everyone here is a mess in one way or another, but most of them figure it out. Eventually."

The words should have been reassuring, but they weren't. Nicola wasn't like the others. She could feel the difference deep inside, in the way her magic responded to the academy's dark energy. The shadows stirred constantly now, slipping through her thoughts like a whisper in the back of her mind. Every time she tried to suppress them, they pushed back, stronger, more insistent.

The pair made their way back towards the main hall, the corridors twisting and turning in ways that felt deliberately confusing. The portraits on the walls seemed to watch them with even more intensity now, their painted eyes following every movement. Nicola avoided looking at them for too long, unsettled by the feeling of being observed. Darkmore Academy was old, older than most magical schools, and it felt like the building itself was a living thing, hiding secrets in every shadow.

When they reached the main hall, a few students were still lingering in small groups, their conversations hushed and cautious. Some carried themselves with a confidence suggesting they had survived this place for a year or more. Others were new arrivals, who, like Nicola, still looked lost and uncertain.

She recognised a few faces from the boat ride, though they seemed different now in the academy's strange light. One young woman was practicing what looked like frost magic, tiny crystals of ice forming and melting in the air around her fingers. A pair of students near the far wall appeared to be arguing in murmurs, their hands occasionally flickering with barely contained energy. Everyone seemed to be wrestling with their own dangerous gifts, their own reasons for having ended up in this place of last resort.

Nicola followed behind Remy as they climbed a set of winding stairs to the upper floors, where the dormitories were located. The stairwell was narrow and steep, the stone steps worn smooth from years of use. Candles floated in the air, casting a flickering glow over the walls, but their light did little to dispel the deepening shadows. The further they climbed, the colder the air became.

"So, are you ready to see your room?" Remy asked as they reached the top of the stairs.

Nicola thought Remy sounded almost excited, though perhaps she was being sarcastic.

"Sure," Nicola replied.

In truth, the thought of staying in this strange place for even one night filled her with dread. She hadn't slept well in months, and she doubted that would change here.

The dormitory hall was long and narrow, lined with heavy wooden doors. Each room was marked by a simple brass number. Remy stopped in front of a door near the end of the hall. Its number was faded, barely visible.

"Here we are," she said. "Room thirteen. Fitting, right?"

Nicola gave a weak smile as the knot of anxiety in her stomach tightened. Thirteen. Of course. The most unlucky number.

Remy pushed the door open with a flourish, revealing a small, sparse room. Nicola cautiously stepped inside. A narrow bed stood against one wall, its thin mattress sagging in the middle. A desk sat in the opposite corner, covered in dust. A single window looked out over the dark, foggy landscape beyond. The room was cold and the air felt thick with something she couldn't quite name.

"I know it's not exactly homey," Remy said,

brushing a hand across the desk, disturbing the layer of dust, "but it's better than some of the other rooms. Trust me."

Nicola's gaze drifted to the corners where the shadows were gathered, thick and impenetrable. The feeling of being watched returned, stronger now, and she couldn't shake the sensation that something – or someone – was hiding in the darkness.

"Don't let the ghosts scare you off," Remy said playfully, leaning against the door frame. "Most of them are harmless. If they show up, just tell them to mind their own business."

The attempt at humour fell flat, but Remy didn't seem to notice. She glanced around the room again, her brow furrowing slightly as if she had been expecting something more.

"I'll let you settle in. Curfew's in about an hour, so don't go wandering around unless you want a lecture from Professor Blackthorn again. She loves an excuse to give those."

Remy turned to leave, but then paused.

"And hey, if you ever want to talk, or whatever,

my dorm room's in the west tower, third floor, right at the end of the hall. It's the one with the old oak door and the little brass owl knocker. You can't miss it."

With that, Remy left, closing the door behind her with a soft click. The silence that followed was almost unpleasant.

Standing alone in the centre of the room, Nicola took a deep breath and let it out slowly, trying to steady herself. This was just another school. Just another place where she didn't belong. But this time, there was no leaving. Darkmore Academy was her last chance. If she couldn't figure out how to control her magic here, she would be out of options.

As much as she tried to push the thought away, she couldn't shake the feeling that this place wanted something from her. The shadows whispered at the edges of her mind, their voices soft and insistent, urging her to let go, to give in.

But she couldn't. Not yet.

Not until she understood what this place truly was.

Chapter Four

Nicola's first night at Darkmore Academy passed in uneasy silence, the kind that gnawed at the edges of her sleep and left her waking every few minutes, disorientated and covered in a cold sweat. Each time she closed her eyes, she dreamt of shadows, shifting and writhing, pulling her deeper into the darkness. It was the same every time – an overwhelming feeling of being consumed by something she couldn't control.

By the time morning arrived, her body ached from tossing and turning, and her mind was clouded with fatigue. The academy's bell tower chimed, its deep, haunting sound echoing through the corridors, signalling the start of the day. She reluctantly pulled herself from the bed, still wearing the clothes she'd arrived in yesterday. When she opened her door to peek outside into the hallway, she found her new uniform folded neatly on the floor – plain, black robes that marked her as a student of the academy. She quickly brought them inside and got changed. Although the material felt coarse and unfamiliar against her skin, there was something almost comforting about the uniformity of it – at least everyone had to dress the same.

Remy was waiting for her in the hallway when she opened her door again. The other students were already bustling about, moving towards their classes.

"You ready for the real fun to begin?" Remy asked, her eyes bright with anticipation.

"Real fun?" Nicola echoed, still tired.

"Classes," Remy replied. "They're... different here. You'll see. Come on, I'll show you where yours is. I've got Advanced Enchantments – a second-year class on the other side of the building. I'll walk with you to your class first, but Professor Brownwing's classroom isn't hard to find once you know the way."

The two of them fell into step with the crowd of students, the flow of bodies moving through the academy's winding corridors. The hallways felt just as confusing in the daylight as they had the night before.

They passed the same portraits, the faces still watching from their frames, but now with expressions that seemed less hostile, as though they had settled into a wary acceptance of Nicola's presence. The academy itself, however, felt just as alive as it had under the cover of darkness. The air hummed with old magic, a steady pulse that thrummed beneath the surface of everything.

"Here you go," Remy said, stopping at a doorway where the walls were lined with shelves full of ancient, dust-covered tomes. "I'll catch up with you at lunch. Try not to let Professor Brownwing intimidate you too much."

Before Nicola could ask any questions, Remy hurried away, the silver beads in her long black hair shimmering faintly as she moved. Without so much as a backward glance, she slipped easily through the crowd of students, heading in the direction of her own class. Watching her disappear, Nicola felt a pang of uncertainty. Remy's effortless confidence – her fluid navigation of the halls, the ease with which she blended into the academy's rhythm – was a stark reminder of how much she herself still had to learn. The winding corridors, the routines, even the very mission of Darkmore Academy felt unfamiliar and vast to Nicola, like an intricate puzzle she wasn't sure how to solve.

Barely managing to brace herself for the unknown, Nicola cautiously stepped into the classroom, her footsteps echoing softly against the wooden floorboards. The room had a low ceiling and narrow windows that barely let in any light. It smelt faintly of mildew and old parchment, as though the air was thick with the weight of centuries-old knowledge.

Professor Brownwing, a thin, stern-looking man with greying hair and sharp eyes, was already at the front of the room. His robes were pristine, an immaculate black. He didn't smile as the students filed in, nor did he acknowledge them beyond a curt nod.

Nicola found an empty desk near the back and quietly slid into the seat, the wooden chair creaking faintly beneath her. She lightly rested her hands on the desk, glancing around at the other students before turning her attention to the front.

As soon as everyone had taken their seats, Professor Brownwing's voice rang out, commanding attention:

"Welcome to Magical Theory and Practice," he said, his tone clipped and formal. "This class is designed to teach you the rules that govern magic. You may think magic is something you can simply wield at your own whim, but here, you will learn the structure, the boundaries. Magic without limits is chaos, and that's what we want to avoid."

Nicola's stomach twisted uncomfortably at his words. The idea of structure, of boundaries, had always felt foreign to her. Her magic didn't fit neatly into any of the categories the other schools had tried to force upon her. It was wild, uncontrollable, and it had always pushed back against the rules they had tried to impose.

"You will learn the foundations of spellwork, the principles that bind magic to the physical world, and the consequences of disobedience," Professor Brownwing continued. "Darkmore Academy does not tolerate those who refuse to understand their limits."

It felt as if Professor Brownwing's words had been meant specifically for her. Nicola could have sworn the other students were watching her, though she knew it was probably just her nerves. She kept her head down, focusing intently on the desk in front of her. The wood was old and scarred, covered in carved symbols and scratches from previous students who had sat here, trying to learn the same lessons she now had to face.

As Professor Brownwing droned on, explaining the history of magical rules and the consequences of breaking them, Nicola's mind drifted back to the shadows that had haunted her dreams. She could still feel them, just beneath the surface of her thoughts.

Consistently precise and sharp, Professor Brownwing's voice didn't waver, but Nicola's mind drifted as the class wore on. She could hear his words, but they felt distant. Her attention slipped away more than once as she struggled to focus. The exhaustion of the strange new environment and her sleepless night pressed down on her, making it difficult to keep up with the intricacies of magical theory.

It wasn't until halfway through the lesson that something shifted.

Professor Brownwing had just begun explaining the process of binding a spell to an object when the air in the room changed. The temperature dropped suddenly, and a faint breeze rustled against the pages of the students' open books. Nicola glanced around, confused that no one else had seemed to notice.

Then, out of the corner of her eye, she saw it – a flicker of movement in the shadows beneath Professor Brownwing's desk. A dark shape, barely more than a ripple in the air, but unmistakably there.

The shadows stretched, shifting and coiling like tendrils, reaching for Professor

Brownwing's legs as he stood there none the wiser, continuing his lecture without pause. The shadows were alive, moving with purpose, and Nicola could feel their pull.

She looked at her classmates, but they were all focused on the lesson, scribbling notes with bored expressions. No one else seemed to see the shadows. No one but her.

The shadows reached further, and for a moment, Nicola thought they would wrap around Professor Brownwing entirely. Her hands clenched into fists under her desk, the familiar sensation of her magic stirring in response to the presence of the shadows. It was like a call, drawing her in, tempting her to join them.

She tried to fight it, tried to suppress the surge of magic rising from within her, but it was no use. The shadows were too strong, their pull too insistent. The edges of her vision blurred, the world around her narrowing to just the activity under Professor Brownwing's desk.

She couldn't hold back any longer.

The shadows responded instantly, twisting

towards her, flowing over the floor like a black tide. She could feel them wrapping around her, filling her senses with cold, suffocating pressure. They were almost hers now, nearly bending to her will, but the power was overwhelming. She could barely breathe under the weight of it.

"Stop," she whispered, her voice trembling.

But the shadows didn't stop. They swirled across the floor, faster, stronger, slipping past her control. Nicola felt a surge of panic as they curled around Professor Brownwing's ankles like living chains. His voice faltered, his eyes narrowing in confusion as he glanced down.

"What the...?"

Before he could finish speaking, the shadows tightened, yanking him off balance. He hit the ground with a thud, papers scattering across the room as the students gasped in shock.

Nicola felt the pull of the magic intensify, her connection to the shadows growing stronger, more desperate. She couldn't stop it. She couldn't control it.

"Release!" Professor Brownwing commanded sharply.

The word cut through the haze of magic, immediately snapping the connection. The shadows recoiled, retreating into the corners of the room, their hold on Nicola slipping away.

Professor Brownwing scrambled to his feet, his expression furious as he scanned the room, his eyes locking onto Nicola. He knew. Somehow, he knew it had been her.

"Class dismissed," he said abruptly, his gaze never leaving Nicola. "Except for you. Stay."

The other students filed out quickly, casting nervous glances Nicola's way as they went.

Professor Brownwing simply looked at Nicola with those sharp eyes, as if trying to peel back the layers of her soul to see what lay beneath. The silence stretched on until it was just the two of them in the room, the tension thick in the air.

"You," he said finally, his voice low and dangerous, "are playing with magic you don't understand."

Chapter Five

Professor Brownwing's eyes burned into Nicola, colder than the shadows she had just lost control of. She shifted in her seat. There was no escaping it now – he knew exactly what had happened. And worse, so did she. Her mouth felt dry, and when she finally spoke, her voice came out hoarse.

"I didn't mean to…"

"That much is clear," Professor Brownwing interrupted, his voice tight with barely restrained anger. "But that's not the point. What happened just then – your lack of control – could have been disastrous."

He took a step closer, looming over Nicola like a storm cloud ready to break. She swallowed hard, trying to find the right words.

"It's just… sometimes it gets away from me."

Professor Brownwing raised an eyebrow, his expression hardening.

"Sometimes?" he said accusingly, glancing down at the floor where the shadows had curled like living things just moments ago. "Think about what just happened. The shadows, your magic – it feeds off chaos, and it thrives in places like this. If you can't control it here, you'll find yourself at the mercy of forces far more dangerous than I am."

His words made Nicola's skin crawl, the truth of them undeniable. She had felt the raw power of the shadows, the way they had pulled at her. She didn't understand them, not fully, but she knew they were connected to something deep, something ancient and dark. Something that could eventually consume her if she wasn't careful.

"I'm trying," she said, hating how small her voice sounded.

"Evidently, you're not trying hard enough."

Silence fell between them, the room pressing down on Nicola as though the very walls were holding their breath, waiting to see what would happen next. Professor Brownwing's gaze remained fixed on her, unblinking, relentless.

"I've seen students like you before," he said finally. "Ones who come here with powerful, unstable magic. Most of them fail. They burn out, or let the magic consume them. They lose control."

Nicola bristled at his words, the sting of them sharp against her already frayed nerves.

"I don't want that to happen to me," she said anxiously.

"Then prove it," said Professor Brownwing.

Nicola stared at him, her hands curling beneath the desk. The shadows stirred at the edges of her vision again, always lurking, waiting for a moment of weakness. She wanted to argue, to defend herself, but deep down, she knew he was right. The shadows were too strong, and she wasn't in control.

Professor Brownwing turned his back to her, pacing the length of the classroom in silence. His robes brushed the floor as he moved, trailing the dust that still lingered in the corners of the room. He didn't speak for a long time, leaving Nicola to sit there in the heavy, uncomfortable quiet.

When he finally stopped, he didn't turn around.

"You're here because you were cast out from other schools, yes?"

"Yes."

"And why was that?"

"Because I couldn't control my magic."

Nicola hated how voicing the truth made it seem all the more real. Every rejection, every expulsion – it had all been because of the same thing. Her power scared people. It scared her.

Professor Brownwing let out a slow breath, as though considering his next words carefully.

"Magic like yours is rare," he said. "It's raw, unrefined, and highly dangerous if mishandled. Most students never encounter anything like it. But here, at Darkmore Academy, we have ways of dealing with such... anomalies."

"Oh?" Nicola uttered curiously.

"There is hope for you yet," Professor Brownwing clarified, though there was a grim note in his voice that made Nicola feel uneasy. "There are things you can do to contain your powers, and if necessary, suppress them."

The idea made Nicola's stomach twist in knots. The thought of her magic – of the shadows – being locked up inside her seemed almost as terrifying as losing control over them. What would be left of her if they were suppressed? Her magic was part of who she was, as twisted and dangerous as it might be.

"Is that what you want me to do?" Nicola asked. "Suppress it?"

Professor Brownwing turned to face her again, his expression unreadable.

"What I want is for you to learn control. How you achieve that is up to you."

"What if I can't?"

"Then you'll be expelled. Permanently."

The word hung in the air like a final verdict. Darkmore Academy was Nicola's last chance. There was no other place for her after this. No more schools, no more training. If she failed here, she wouldn't just be cast out from the magical world – she would be a danger to it.

Her mind raced. She had been so focused on surviving, on keeping her head down and avoiding attention, but it was now clear that wasn't enough. The shadows were growing stronger, more insistent, and if she didn't find a way to control them soon, she would be entirely on her own.

"I understand," she said quietly, a hint of shame lacing her tone.

Professor Brownwing watched her for a moment longer, then nodded, his expression softening ever so slightly.

"Good," he said. "I won't hesitate to remove you if you pose a threat to this academy – or to yourself."

Nicola swallowed the lump in her throat, trying to push down the rising panic.

"What do I need to do?"

"You need to learn the boundaries of your magic. Right now, your power is chaotic because you lack the discipline to control it, but there are methods you can pursue."

"Methods?" Nicola uttered cautiously.

"There are spells, rituals, even meditations designed to help. However, they come with risks. The magic you wield can attract attention – dangerous attention. It's not just about controlling your own power. There are forces in this world that are drawn to it, and if you're not careful, you may invite something far worse than chaos."

Nicola's blood ran cold. She had already felt it – the pull of the shadows, the way they seemed to respond to something beyond her. The whispers in her dreams, the flickers of movement at the edges of her vision... it wasn't just her magic. Something else was lurking, waiting, and she had no idea how close it was to breaking through.

"I'll do whatever it takes," she said, trying to keep the fear from her voice. "I can't let this control me anymore."

"Then you'd better start working. Before it's too late."

The professor turned away from her again, this time heading towards the door. His robes swirled around him as he moved, a silent, graceful motion that reminded her of the shadows themselves.

"I suggest you begin in the library," he said over his shoulder as he reached for the door handle. "There are texts there that might help you. But tread carefully. The library has a reputation for leading students astray."

As Professor Brownwing opened the door, air from the hallway swept into the classroom. Nicola stared at his back, her mind racing with a thousand questions, but none of them seemed to matter now. The only thing that mattered was control.

Without another word, the professor left, the door closing behind him with a dull thud. Nicola sat there for a long moment, the silence pressing down on her. The idea of wandering into a labyrinth of old books in search of answers felt like just another risk. But what choice did she have? She couldn't afford to fail.

With a deep breath, she pushed herself up from her seat, her legs feeling weak beneath her. The shadows were still there, lingering at the edges of her vision. Although they seemed a little quieter now, she knew she couldn't trust them to stay that way.

She needed to get stronger. She needed to understand what she was dealing with.

And she needed to do it fast.

School of Misfits

Chapter Six

The library loomed ahead – a dark, silent cathedral at the heart of Darkmore Academy. It was larger than Nicola had imagined, its stone walls rising up like the ribs of a beast, disappearing into the shadows high above. The entrance was guarded by two massive wooden doors, carved with ancient symbols that pulsed faintly with magic. A dim light flickered from within, casting long shadows across the floor as she approached.

The hallway was deserted, the air thick with the weight of untold secrets and forgotten knowledge. The few students she had passed on her way had given the library a wide berth, as if they knew better than to venture inside without a clear purpose. Nicola had heard the whispers, even in the short time she had been here. The library had a reputation as an ever-shifting maze of books and scrolls that had led more than one student to lose their way. Some said it was cursed, others claimed it was haunted, but no one seemed to agree on exactly what made it so dangerous.

All she knew was that it held answers. Answers she needed.

The doors creaked as Nicola pushed them open. The library was enormous, its shelves stretching far beyond what her eyes could see, filled with books of every size and shape, some bound in leather, others in materials she couldn't recognise. The ceiling was high, supported by stone arches that crisscrossed above, and the smell of old parchment and ink filled the air, mingling with something else – something faintly metallic, like the scent of a storm about to break.

As Nicola stepped inside, the heavy doors closed behind her, loud and foreboding. For a moment, she stood there, letting her eyes adjust to the dim light. The shadows in the nearby corners seemed to shift slightly, almost as if they were aware of her presence.

But she didn't have time to be afraid. Not now.

Professor Brownwing's words echoed in her mind: *The library has a reputation for leading students astray.*

Whatever that meant, she would deal with it. The risk was worth it if she could find something – anything – that would help her control her magic. The library held knowledge that wasn't taught in regular classes, texts that dealt with the darker, more dangerous aspects of magic. Nicola needed that knowledge, even if it came with a price.

She moved deeper into the library, her eyes scanning the shelves as she passed. The titles of some of the books were written in languages she didn't recognise, some faded with age, others glowing faintly with runes that twinkled in the low light. A few books seemed to hum with magic, almost trembling as though the words inside were eager to escape.

It was overwhelming. Nicola didn't know where to start. The sheer volume of information was staggering, and the idea of wandering aimlessly, hoping to stumble across something useful, filled her with a sense of helplessness.

Focus, she told herself. She needed to narrow her search.

The shadows around her flickered again, responding to her rising anxiety. She took a deep breath, trying to calm herself, but the feeling of being watched grew stronger. The library felt alive, as though it was aware of her presence.

She turned down a narrow aisle between two towering bookshelves, her fingers trailing along the spines of the books as she walked. Some of them were cracked and crumbling, their pages yellowed with age, while others were pristine, as though they had never been touched. Her hand hovered over a thick, black volume that seemed to hum with a low, insistent energy. She hesitated. Something about it felt wrong, like it was waiting for her to open it.

She pulled her hand away, moving on.

Time passed in a blur of shelves and books, and still she found nothing. The deeper into the library she went, the darker it became, the dim light from the entrance having long faded behind her. The shelves here were older, the books dustier, their spines brittle and worn. The shadows gathered more thickly in this part of the library, swirling in the corners like living things, watching her with invisible eyes.

She was about to turn back, a sense of failure pressing down on her, when a voice broke the silence.

"Looking for something?"

Nicola froze, her heart leaping into her throat. The voice was soft and feminine, barely more than a whisper, but it sent a chill down her spine. Slowly, she turned towards the source of the sound.

A figure stepped out from between the shelves, cloaked in darkness. It was a young woman, about Nicola's age, with long pale hair that shimmered ever so faintly. Her skin was almost translucent, as though she were made of the very mist that clung to the academy's exterior. There was something unsettling about her presence, something that made the air feel colder.

"Who are you?" Nicola asked, her voice trembling.

"Someone like you," the young woman replied with a smile that didn't quite reach her eyes.

The answer didn't comfort Nicola. In fact, it only deepened her feeling of unease.

"I don't know what you mean," Nicola said.

The young woman tilted her head, her pale eyes gleaming.

"You're looking for control, aren't you?" she said knowingly. "Over your magic. Over the shadows."

"How do you know that?" Nicola asked, her posture stiffening.

"I've seen others like you," the young woman said, stepping closer, her movements unnaturally smooth as though she was gliding over the floor rather than walking. "Students who come here, lost, desperate, seeking control over powers they can't handle."

The words sent a jolt of recognition through Nicola. They were too precise, too familiar.

"What are you?" Nicola asked, the question slipping out before she could stop herself.

The woman smiled again, this time wider, showing too many teeth.

"I'm what you could become, if you're not careful."

"What do you mean?" Nicola demanded fearfully.

"This place is more than just a school," said the woman, her eyes darkening and the shadows around her thickening. "It's alive. It feeds off students like you, ones with magic too wild to be tamed. The academy will either break you or use you."

The words hit Nicola like a punch to the gut. She had felt it since the moment she'd arrived – the pull of the academy, the way it seemed to demand something from her. The fear that had been gnawing at her was finally starting to make sense, taking form in a way she could no longer ignore.

"You're lying," she said, not wanting to believe it, though her voice wavered.

"Am I?" said the woman, her smile fading. "You can feel it, can't you? The academy's magic. It's everywhere. Watching. Waiting."

Nicola took a step back, her hands trembling. The shadows around her seemed to pulse, matching the rhythm of her own. She wanted to run, to get away from this strange woman, but her feet felt rooted to the floor.

"If you want to survive here," the woman continued, "you need to learn control. Not just over your magic, but over the academy itself."

"How is that even possible?" Nicola asked.

"There's a book. A forbidden text hidden deep in the library. It holds the knowledge you need, the spells that will teach you to control the shadows. But it's dangerous. More dangerous than anything you've encountered so far."

Nicola hesitated, doubt gnawing at her. A forbidden book? It sounded like the exact thing she had been warned against, the kind of dark magic that could lead her astray. But at the same time, she felt the pull of it – the promise of control over her powers.

"It's your only chance," said the woman, her voice still soft, but insistent. "Without it, the academy will consume you."

Nicola swallowed hard. Could she really trust this woman? Was this some kind of trap, a test set by the academy to see how far she would go?

But as she stood there, the shadows swirling around her, she realised she didn't have a choice. She couldn't keep going like this, fighting against magic she didn't understand. If there was a way to control it, even if it was dangerous, she had to try.

"Where is it?" she asked, her voice steady now.

The young woman smiled a slow, cold smile.

"Follow me."

Chapter Seven

The silence between them stretched on as the young woman led Nicola deeper into the library. Nicola wasn't sure how long they had been walking. Time felt different here, like it slowed the further they went. Each step felt heavier than the last, as though the very air was pushing against her, trying to stop her from going any further. But she didn't stop. She couldn't. Not now, when she was perhaps that vital bit closer to finding the answers she needed.

At last, they came to a stop at a section so deep and hidden that it felt to Nicola as though they had stepped into another world entirely. The shelves here were taller, towering over them like ancient sentinels, and the books were bound in an unusual, dark leather that glistened in the faint light.

"This is it," the strange woman said.

Nicola turned to look at one of the shelves. The books hummed with a low, dangerous energy, as though the knowledge inside them was too powerful to be contained. She reached out, her fingers trembling slightly as they brushed against a spine.

It felt somehow different from what she had been expecting, the cover smooth and worn, centuries old. An eerily familiar magic thrummed beneath her fingertips, but something about it felt wrong. The magic wasn't just powerful – it was hungry, as if the book was waiting for someone to open it, to unleash whatever it was that was inside.

"That's the one," said the young woman. "It's interesting that you seem to have been drawn to it. The magic on those pages is nothing like the magic you've studied before. It's older, darker. It will take more from you than you realise."

Nicola hesitated, her hand hovering over the book. She could feel the shadows stirring within her, pulling her towards the magic like moths to a flame. The hunger inside her was undeniable – she needed this power. She needed control. But the young woman's warning hung over her like a heavy shroud.

"What will it take from me?" Nicola asked, struggling to keep her voice steady.

"Everything, if you let it," said the woman.

The words sent a jolt of fear through Nicola, but she didn't pull her hand away. She knew the risks – such was the danger of working with unstable magic. The academy, Professor Brownwing, even her own instincts – they had all warned her that nothing about her magic was simple. Control wasn't something that would come easily.

And yet, here she was. On the edge of something powerful, something that might finally give her the control she had been searching for.

With a deep breath, Nicola pulled the book from the shelf.

The weight of it settled in her hands. The leather cover felt slick beneath her fingers, as though it had been soaked in some kind of strange, oily substance. There were no markings on the outside, no title, no indication of what lay within. But the magic that pulsed from it was unmistakable – foreboding, ancient, and alive.

"Open it," the young woman urged, her voice soft but insistent.

Nicola's fingers trembled as she lifted the cover to reveal the first page. The parchment was yellowed with age, the ink faded but still legible. Strange symbols and runes filled the page, swirling and twisting in patterns that seemed to shift and move as she looked at them. The language was unfamiliar, something old and forgotten, but as she stared at the words, a startling clarity began to form in her mind.

She could understand them!

Her breath caught in her throat as the symbols began to glow faintly, pulsing in a consistent, subtle rhythm. The magic in the book was reaching out to her, curling around her thoughts like a living thing, whispering promises of power and control. The shadows within her responded, stirring with a new energy, eager to connect with the magic on the page.

"Focus," the woman said, stepping closer. "Let the magic in. It will show you the way."

In some ways, Nicola wanted to pull back, to close the book and walk away, but the pull was too strong. The magic was already inside her, winding through her mind, her soul, binding itself to the shadows that had always been a part of her. It felt right – like she had been waiting for this moment all her life.

Her vision blurred as the symbols on the page began to shift, forming into new shapes, new patterns. The words rearranged themselves, revealing something deeper, something hidden beneath the surface. It wasn't just a spell – it was a ritual. A way to bind herself to the shadows, to control them in a way she had never imagined to be possible.

But there had to be a catch. She could feel it in the way the magic tugged at her, pulling her deeper into its embrace.

"You see it now, don't you?" the woman said triumphantly. "The way forward."

Nicola nodded, unable to tear her eyes away from the page. The ritual was complex, requiring precision and deep engagement, but it was possible. She could do this. She could control the shadows, bend them to her will. She just had to follow the steps and perform the ritual exactly as it was written.

The only problem was the final line of the text – written in bold, jagged script at the bottom of the page. Indeed, it was a warning.

The shadows require balance. The price for control is steep. Beware the cost.

Nicola's heart raced as she read the words again, their enormity sinking in. The price for control. She didn't know what that meant yet, but one thing was certain: once she began, there would be no turning back.

"You're afraid," the woman said knowingly.

Nicola swallowed hard, the taste of fear sharp on her tongue.

"Shouldn't I be?"

"Fear is just another barrier to be overcome," the woman said with an almost menacing smile. "If you let it stop you, you'll never find the control you're looking for."

The woman's logic made sense, but it did nothing to ease Nicola's worries. The fear was still there, gnawing at the edges of her mind. There was so much riding on this and so much that could go wrong.

Nicola quickly closed the book, causing the pages to press together. The ritual was still burned into her mind, the steps clear and precise. She knew what she had to do, despite the doubts that lingered in the back of her thoughts, a torment she couldn't shake.

"So," said the woman, watching Nicola closely, "what will you do?"

Nicola took a deep breath, her fingers tightening around the book.

"I'll do what I have to."

"Indeed," said the woman, her smile widening as something dangerous flickered in her eyes. "I hope you're ready for whatever comes next."

Without another word, the mysterious woman turned and disappeared, her pale figure fading into the darkness like mist dissolving in the night.

The silence that followed the woman's departure was almost overbearing. Nicola stood alone, clutching the strange book in her hands. The shadows around her shifted, restless and keen, as though they could sense the change in her. She had the opportunity now – the knowledge. But with it came responsibility, and the risk of what might happen if she failed.

Beware the cost.

The words echoed in Nicola's mind as she turned and made her way back through the maze of bookshelves. She had no idea what the consequences would be, but she had already made her choice.

Chapter Eight

The air felt different when Nicola stepped out of the library. Heavier, thicker, as though the very atmosphere was aware of the book she was carrying. The weight of it in her hands was more than physical now; it pressed against her mind, whispering promises of power with every step she took. The shadows around her were restless, shifting at the edges of her vision, but she kept her focus forward, pushing down the gnawing unease that clung to her.

The academy was quieter than usual, the hallways nearly deserted. Most of the students were already in their dorm rooms, the bell for curfew having rung some time ago. The few who remained scurried past Nicola, not daring to look her in the eye. Maybe they sensed it – the change in her. Or maybe they were just as afraid of this place as she was.

Nicola made her way back to her room. Subtle but impossible to ignore, the book's magic vibrated through her fingers. It was alive, just like the shadows within her, and they were both waiting for her to make her move.

The door to her dorm room creaked as she pushed it open. As soon as her feet crossed the threshold, she closed the door behind her; the need for privacy was paramount. The space was just as cold and dark as it had been the night before, but now, with the book in her hands, the room felt different – more alive, more aware. The shadows stirred in response to the presence of the book, curling along the walls, eager for what was to come.

Nicola placed the book on the desk, her fingers brushing over its worn cover. The ritual was clear in her mind, each step etched into her thoughts with perfect clarity. She had never performed anything like it before – nothing this dangerous, nothing this powerful. But she had no choice now. If she wanted control, she had to take it.

The warning at the bottom of the page flickered in her memory: *The price for control is steep. Beware the cost.*

Her breath came in shallow bursts as she opened the book to the page where the ritual was written. The ancient symbols glowed faintly in the dim light, their magic already beginning to weave itself into the air.

Nicola hesitated for a moment, her hand hovering over the first line of the text. Fear gnawed at her, as did the uncertainty of what this ritual would demand from her, but the pull of the shadows was stronger. She could feel them inside her, restless.

With a deep breath, she began.

The first step was simple: a chant, ancient and rhythmic, designed to open a connection between herself and the shadows. The words rolled off her tongue, foreign but familiar, as though they had been buried deep within her all along. The magic responded immediately, the shadows around her thickening, swirling like a living storm, drawn to the power of the ritual.

Her hands moved over the book, tracing the symbols as she chanted. The air in the room grew colder, the shadows pressing in closer. They reached for her, curling around her fingers, her wrists, slipping up her arms like tendrils of smoke. She could feel their hunger, their need for connection. She let them in, allowing the darkness to flow through her.

As the ritual progressed, the shadows became stronger, more insistent. They whispered in her ears, their voices soft and seductive, promising power beyond anything she had ever known. She could feel them pressing against the edges of her mind, trying to push their way inside, but she held them back, keeping just enough control to guide the ritual.

The next step required blood.

Nicola hesitated again, the enormity of what she was about to do settling heavily on her. Blood magic was forbidden in most schools, and for good reason. It required a sacrifice – one that was often greater than anyone was willing to pay. But the ritual demanded it, and if she wanted to succeed, she had to follow it to the letter.

She assessed the items scattered across her desk – old quills, loose papers, and a small sewing kit. Inside it lay a single silver needle, glinting innocently in the faint light. With trembling fingers, she picked it up, its point perfectly sharp.

The shadows around her pulsed, urging her forward. They wanted this. They *needed* this.

Taking a steadying breath, Nicola pressed the needle into the tip of her finger – a sharp pinprick of pain. A single drop of blood welled up, glistening crimson. She allowed it to slowly drip onto the pages of the book, staining the ancient parchment with her sacrifice. The shadows reacted instantly, hungrily wrapping themselves around her like a living cloak.

The pain in Nicola's finger faded into the background as she continued the ritual, the words flowing from her lips faster now, the magic intensifying with every syllable. The shadows within her were growing stronger, more solid, their presence overwhelming. She could feel them merging with her, becoming a part of her in a way they never had before. The power was intoxicating, flooding her senses with raw energy, and for the first time in her life, she felt like she was in control.

But something was wrong.

As the ritual neared its end, the shadows began to change. They weren't just a part of her anymore – they were truly *inside* her, seeping into her mind, her soul. The connection was too deep, too strong. Nicola quickly realised, albeit too late, that the magic was taking more from her than she had anticipated. The shadows weren't just bending to her will – they were *becoming* her will.

Her heartbeat quickened, panic rising in her chest. She tried to pull back, to end the ritual prematurely, but the shadows wouldn't let go. They had sunk their claws into her, wrapping themselves around her thoughts, her memories, twisting and reshaping them. The whispers grew louder, more insistent, drowning out her own thoughts, until she couldn't tell where they ended and she began.

As the final words of the ritual escaped her lips, the shadows surged violently, consuming her entirely. The room around her disappeared, swallowed by the darkness, and for a moment, there was nothing but the cold, suffocating pressure of the shadows pushing down on her from all sides.

Then, just as suddenly as it had begun, the ritual ended.

The shadows receded, slipping away like acrid smoke, leaving Nicola gasping for breath. The room came into focus again, the shadows no longer swirling in restless patterns. The air felt still, quiet, as though a storm had passed.

But something was different.

Nicola looked down at her hands, expecting to see blood still beading on her fingertip, but the tiny wound had already sealed, leaving only the faintest mark. The book lay open on the desk, the symbols on the page no longer glowing, their magic spent.

Of all the changes, the most noticeable one was in her.

She could feel the shadows inside her, not just lurking at the edges of her mind, but fully integrated into her being. They were no longer something separate. They were a part of her now, woven into the very fabric of who she was. Something felt off about it.

She could still hear the whispers. Faint, distant, but always there, just beneath the surface of her thoughts. If the shadows *had* just given her power – they had clearly taken something from her in return. Something she couldn't quite put into words, but something vital, something human.

Doubt began to gnaw at her, a persistent whisper in the back of her mind. Had she been too hasty in trusting the strange young woman in the library? Her unsettling presence had felt both alluring and dangerous, but now, in the quiet aftermath of the ritual, Nicola's instincts clawed at her.

Professor Brownwing's warning echoed through her thoughts like an ominous chant. *The library has a reputation for leading students astray.* Perhaps she had been foolish to assume that the stranger in the library truly had her best interests at heart. The professor had urged caution, and yet, in the moment, Nicola had been so captivated by the promise of power that she had ignored his advice.

Nicola recalled the ghostly woman's smile, the way she had spoken of the book with such reverence. But was that reverence genuine? Or had it been a façade to mask something far more sinister? It was entirely plausible that not all entities tied to Darkmore Academy were benevolent. The academy thrummed with a dark history, and Nicola was now acutely aware that she might have opened a door that could never be closed. The uncertainty clawed at her, a reminder that the line between ally and enemy could easily blur in this bleak, unnerving place.

Doubt wormed its way deeper into her thoughts, twisting and turning. What if the young woman in the library had meant well? Perhaps she had seen something in Nicola – a spark of potential or innocent desperation – and had genuinely wanted to help. Maybe it was the book that couldn't be trusted. After all, it radiated an energy that seemed almost malevolent, as if it held secrets that were never meant to be unearthed. What if the woman had unknowingly recommended something far beyond her comprehension?

Nicola pressed her palms against her

temples, her bewilderment and frustration close to boiling point. She had followed the ritual's instructions with utmost care, every step meticulously memorised. And yet, what if she had misinterpreted something? Maybe in her eagerness, she had overlooked a crucial detail, an incantation or a more specific warning hidden within the lines of the ancient text. She had thought she felt confident, empowered even, but now that certainty felt like a distant memory, slipping through her fingers like sand.

What if she had invited something she couldn't control, a darkness that would wrap around her and squeeze until there was nothing left?

Stealing her solitude, there was a sharp knock at her door, shattering the quiet. Irritation bubbled up inside her. She was just about to tell whoever it was to go away when the door swung open to reveal a familiar face.

"Are you alright?" Remy asked. "You look like you've seen a ghost."

"I'm fine," Nicola lied, her voice steady but hollow.

Remy raised an eyebrow, her gaze flicking to the book on the desk. Nicola could sense it: Remy knew exactly what the book was and the powerful magic it held. There was a knowing look in her eyes, a silent recognition that made Nicola's skin prickle with horror.

Remy then looked at Nicola for a long, uncomfortable moment.

Following the awkward silence, Remy finally turned and walked away. Nicola felt an immense wave of relief wash over her, her shoulders slackening. Listening intently, she waited until the sound of Remy's footsteps had faded completely.

Satisfied that the coast was clear, Nicola moved quickly. She shoved the book into her desk drawer, as though she could hide its presence from both herself and everyone else. Even with the drawer closed, however, something about sharing her space with such a strange book, the thought of sleeping with it mere feet away, sent a chill through her. She didn't fancy the alternative though; she shuddered at the thought of taking the book back to the library. The ancient shelves, filled with dark secrets and hidden knowledge –

and the mysterious young woman who had directed her – were just as unnerving, if not more so. No, the book would stay here. She couldn't face the library, not now.

Chapter Nine

The next few days passed in a blur. The academy continued its usual rhythm, classes and curfews, but for Nicola, everything had shifted. The shadows inside her felt heavier than ever, their whispers constant, always at the edge of her thoughts. They were entirely a part of her now, woven into the very essence of her being.

She could feel their increasing appetite, gnawing at her insides like a void that could never be filled. It had started the moment she completed the ritual, and though she had gained perhaps some extent of control over her magic, it was far from perfect. The shadows were always there, always pulling, waiting for her to lose focus, waiting for a moment of weakness.

In class, Nicola kept her head down, trying

to stay unnoticed, but it was harder now. The power inside her was stronger than ever, and no matter how hard she tried to suppress it, it leaked out in small, subtle ways. The shadows trailed behind her in dark tendrils as she moved, flickering at the edges of her vision. The other students began to notice, their glances more frequent, their whispers more pointed.

Even the professors seemed to be watching her more closely. Their eyes followed her with a blend of suspicion and curiosity, though none of them had said anything – yet. Nicola could feel the tension in the air, the unspoken understanding that something had changed, something that couldn't be explained.

Remy, however, seemed completely unfazed by the growing strangeness. If anything, she seemed even more interested in Nicola now, following her with that same sharp, knowing smile. Remy was always there, just at the edge of every conversation, every moment, like a shadow herself. Although she had been a strange comfort to Nicola at first, her presence now felt more unsettling than reassuring.

One night, as Nicola lay in bed, staring at the ceiling, her mind raced with the memories of the ritual and the whispers of the shadows that had followed. The words of the forbidden book still echoed in her thoughts, the warning about the cost of control now more tangible than ever.

She sat up and swung her legs over the side of the bed. She couldn't sleep, not with the shadows this close, this loud. She needed air – space to think. To breathe.

Without a second thought, she changed into her day clothes, fastening the buttons with hurried fingers. She then put on her shoes, the leather stiff as she buckled them. Finally, she grabbed her cloak, draping it over her shoulders before slipping out of her room, careful not to wake anyone in the rooms nearby. The corridor was silent, the other students evidently asleep.

She made her way through the halls towards the academy's courtyard. When she stepped outside, the night air hit her like a wave. The fog that constantly surrounded the academy was thicker tonight, swirling in slow, lazy patterns around the spires of the building.

The moon was hidden behind a blanket of clouds, casting everything in a dull, silvery glow. There was nobody else around; it was peaceful, save for the faint rustle of the wind against the ivy-covered walls.

For a moment, Nicola just stood there, breathing in the cold air, letting it wash over her. The shadows were still with her, but here, outside, they felt less oppressive. The open space gave her a brief sense of freedom, though she knew it wouldn't last. The hunger of the shadows inside her was growing, and no amount of fresh air could quench it.

She walked across the courtyard, her footsteps soft on the cobblestones, and found herself drawn to the far side of the grounds where the academy's oldest tower stood. The tower was crumbling, its stone walls covered in thick vines and moss, its windows murky and dull. It had been abandoned centuries ago, according to the stories, and no one went near it. Not even the professors.

But tonight, something about it called to her.

Nicola's feet moved before she had time to think, carrying her towards the tower. The shadows inside her pulsed with excitement, their whispers growing louder as she approached. The air around the tower felt different to the rest of the courtyard, and she could feel the magic here – old, ancient magic, thick in the air like smoke. It brushed over her skin like chalk dust.

The door to the tower was slightly ajar, the wood rotted and worn from years of neglect. She pushed it open slowly, the hinges groaning in protest as she stepped inside. The musty scent of decay and dust filled her lungs as she moved deeper into the tower. The shadows clung to the walls, thicker here, darker, as though they had been waiting for her.

The tower was still, its halls long abandoned, but Nicola could feel something here – something watching. The magic in the air was palpable, humming beneath the surface like a living thing. The shadows inside her stirred restlessly, keen to explore, to uncover whatever secrets were hidden close by.

She moved carefully through the narrow halls, her footsteps echoing softly in the stillness. The further she went, the more the shadows seemed to pull her, guiding her deeper into the heart of the tower. She didn't know what she was looking for, but the feeling of something ancient, something powerful, drew her forward.

Finally, Nicola reached a spiral staircase that wound up towards the top of the tower. The steps were crumbling, covered in moss and dirt, but she climbed them slowly, one hand trailing along the cool stone wall for balance. The shadows swirled around her, their whispers growing more insistent with every step.

At the top of the stairs, she found herself in a small circular room. The walls were lined with faded tapestries, their colours long since drained by time. The floor was covered in a thick layer of dust. At the centre of the room was a pedestal, and on it lay a single object – a modestly-sized black mirror.

The shadows around her seemed to surge forward, drawn to the mirror with a kind of magnetic pull. Nicola's heart raced as she stepped closer, the air around her growing heavier, suffocating almost. The mirror was no ordinary object – she could feel its power, its connection to the shadows, to the magic she had been struggling to control.

Her reflection wavered in the dark glass, warped by the magic emanating from it. As she drew closer, the shadows within her stirred, their whispers swelling into a restless chorus. They craved this. They demanded it.

Nicola reached out, her hand trembling.

She touched the surface of the mirror, and immediately, the cold hit her like a shock, causing a wave of icy energy to surge through her body. The shadows inside her exploded, rushing forward. The room around her disappeared, swallowed by the darkness, and for a moment, there was nothing but a frigid, bleak void.

And then, the whispers stopped.

She stood frozen in place, her hand still resting on the surface of the mirror, her breath shallow and ragged. The shadows had gone silent, their presence still there, but no longer pressing against her thoughts. The hunger had faded. It had been replaced by something else – something deeper, more powerful.

Control.

Nicola pulled her hand away from the mirror, her chest heaving as she tried to catch her breath. The room was still the same, the shadows still thick and heavy around her, but now, she sensed she was in control. The power she had felt since the ritual had settled – it was no longer wild and chaotic, but focused.

However, she now understood the cost of this control.

The shadows were hers, but they were also something more. They were part of the academy, part of the ancient magic that lived within these walls, and by having accepted them, she had bound herself to it.

She felt so alive, but there was an uncertainty that gnawed at her.

Chapter Ten

The night air hit Nicola as she stepped out of the tower. Instead of feeling the usual chill, she felt invigorated. The shadows inside her were quiet now, humming softly beneath the surface, completely under her control. The hunger that had gnawed at her for days had settled to be replaced by a sense of calm she hadn't felt in a long time.

She stood in the courtyard for a moment, letting what had just happened settle over her. The mirror in the tower had changed something inside her, something fundamental. She could feel it in the way the shadows responded to her now. They were no longer wild and unpredictable, but obedient, like they were waiting for her next command.

For the first time since arriving at Darkmore

Academy, Nicola felt like she belonged. Not just to the school itself, but to the magic. The darkness, the ancient power that flowed through the walls of this place – it was a part of her now, and she was a part of it. The realisation was both terrifying and exhilarating.

She knew deep down that although she had gained control, the cost was clear – she was now bound to the academy. But for now, she didn't care. The power coursing through her veins was intoxicating, and the control she had longed for was finally hers.

The academy was quiet as Nicola made her way back to her dorm. The shadows followed her in silence, but now they moved with purpose, no longer chaotic or hungry. They were hers to command.

When Nicola reached her room, she was startled to find Remy sitting on her bed, having let herself in. Remy's usual playful smirk was absent and had been replaced by something sharper, more serious. The subtle moonlight from the window cast long shadows across Remy's face, emphasising the worry etched into her features. In that moment, Nicola sensed that Remy was deeply attuned to everything that had been happening, her investment palpable and intense.

"You've been busy," Remy said, her voice low.

"You could say that," Nicola said as she closed the door behind her, her pulse quickening.

Remy's gaze lingered on Nicola for a moment.

"You've changed," she said. "I can see it."

Nicola didn't respond, but Remy was right. She had changed. The ritual, the mirror, the shadows – they had all shifted something inside her. She wasn't the same person she had been when she arrived at the academy, and she wasn't sure if that was a good thing or not.

"You need to be careful," Remy continued, her voice soft but insistent. "The magic you've tapped into – it's not just about control. It's about survival. The academy... it feeds off students like you. And now that you've unlocked this, it's going to want more."

"What do you mean, 'want more'?" Nicola asked, her voice tight.

"The academy is like a living thing," Remy explained. "It gives power, but it takes just as much. Students who come here with strong magic – especially the ones who tap into the older, darker forces – often suffer greatly. The academy tests them, pushes them, until they either break or become something else entirely."

Nicola's heart raced as she processed Remy's words. She had always known there was something off about this place, but hearing it spoken aloud by a more experienced student made it feel all too real.

"Why didn't you tell me this sooner?" Nicola asked, her voice trembling with a blend of frustration and fear.

"I thought you'd figure it out on your own," Remy said. "And besides, I assumed you could handle it. You're stronger than the others. I've seen it."

Nicola felt a flicker of something – gratitude, maybe – but it was quickly swallowed by a growing sense of unease.

"What do I do now?" she asked, her voice small, uncertain.

"You keep going," Remy said with a sigh, crossing her arms over her chest. "You learn to balance it, but you have to be careful. The more power you take, the more the academy will take from you in return. If you don't find that balance, it'll consume you."

The words hit Nicola like a blow, the reality of her situation settling in with terrifying clarity. She had the power she wanted – the shadows were hers now – but they were also part of something much bigger, something she didn't fully understand yet.

"Is that what happened to you?" Nicola asked. "Is that why you're so... at ease with the macabre?"

Remy's eyes flickered with something. Nicola couldn't quite tell if it was regret, understanding, or perhaps a mixture of both.

"I've been here long enough to know the rules," said Remy. "I've seen enough students fall victim to the academy's magic to know that the only way to survive is to play by its rules."

Nicola wanted to ask more, to push for answers, but something in Remy's expression told her not to. Whatever secrets Remy carried, they were too deep, too painful to unearth in a single conversation.

Instead, Nicola nodded.

"I'll be careful," she said stoically.

"Good," said Remy, offering a small smile. "Because I'd hate to see the academy take you."

Remy stood up from the bed. She hesitated for a moment, her gaze lingering on Nicola as if searching for the right words. But with a slight nod, she opened the door, stepped out into the hallway, and began walking away.

As Nicola sat down on the edge of her bed, the weight of the shadows settled over her again, but this time, she didn't fight it. She let them in, let them wrap around her like a cloak, their presence both comforting and unnerving. Yes, she had the control she needed, but seemingly, the academy – this living being of an academy – was still waiting, expecting something from her.

Chapter Eleven

It was as though the academy had been watching Nicola all along, waiting for her to cross that invisible line. And now, she had. The days passed in a strange blur. Her classes felt distant, like a distraction from the real challenges. She found herself avoiding the other students more and more, keeping her head down, keeping the shadows close. Remy had tried to reach out a few times, but even their conversations felt strained, as though they both feared what was coming, but were afraid to speak it aloud.

The academy wasn't going to let Nicola off lightly.

Late one night, as she lay in bed, something shifted. It was subtle at first, barely more than a whisper at the edge of her senses, but she felt it. The shadows inside her stirred, restless and alert, as if something had called to them. She sat up, her breath catching in her throat as the room seemed to darken around her, the corners of the walls slipping out of focus.

The academy was testing her, she knew it.

The shadows began to move on their own, swirling around her bed like a living storm. She tried to reach for them, to pull them back under her control, but they slipped through her fingers, sliding out of her grasp like smoke. The magic was still there, still a part of her, but it was different now. The academy was pushing, pressing, trying to break her will. She wanted to scream. Despite what she might have felt before, she hadn't won at all.

She stood abruptly, her bare feet quickly marching her towards the door. But as soon as she touched the handle, the walls of the room shifted. The door, once solid and real, seemed to flicker and fade, dissolving into nothingness as if it had never even been there.

Panic surged in Nicola's chest, but she fought it down. This was an illusion. It had to be.

The academy was playing with her, bending the very walls of reality, testing her limits. It was as though it wanted her to lose her mind so it could take her over completely.

Nicola closed her eyes, forcing herself to focus. The shadows were hers. They were a part of her, even if the academy was twisting them against her now. She had to remember that. They were bound to her, and as much as the academy wanted to push her, somewhere deep down, she believed she could still take control.

Refusing to be beaten, she slowly opened her eyes, fixing her attention on the centre of the room. The shadows danced at the edges of her vision, but she told herself to stay calm. The academy was testing her, but that didn't mean she had to succumb.

With a deep breath, she took a step forward, then another. The room around her seemed to pulse, the walls warping and shifting like liquid, but she didn't stop. She couldn't. Each step felt heavier than the last, like the very air was trying to hold her in place, but she kept moving.

The shadows pressed in closer, swirling faster now, their whispers growing louder, more insistent. They wanted her to give in, to let go, but she clenched her fists in defiance. She had to stay in control. She had to stay *herself*.

As she moved deeper into the illusion, the academy's presence grew stronger, more demanding. The walls around her blurred and twisted, no longer recognisable as part of her room. Instead, they became something different, something older. The shadows deepened, turning into figures – vague, distorted shapes, watching her with hollow, empty eyes.

They weren't real. They couldn't be.

But as Nicola stood determined, one of the figures moved closer towards her. It slid out of the shadows, its form taking shape into a figure tall and thin, with a face shrouded in darkness. The air around the figure crackled with magic. As it moved closer still, Nicola could feel the weight of its presence pressing against her.

She stumbled back, her breath catching as the figure reached out, its hand extending towards her. But it didn't touch her. It hovered there, just inches away, its fingers curling menacingly as if to beckon her forward.

"You are one of us now," the figure whispered, its voice like the wind through dead trees.

"No," Nicola whispered shakily. "I'm not."

The figure's hand moved closer, almost touching Nicola's skin.

"You belong to the shadows. You belong to this place."

"*I* control the shadows," Nicola said, forcing herself to stand her ground. "They don't control me."

The figure's eyes began to glow a deep yellow, piercing through the darkness shrouding its face. For a moment, the shadows around Nicola seemed to flicker, shifting in response to the figure's unsettling gaze.

Nicola didn't back down. She couldn't. With a slow, deliberate breath, she searched deep within herself and called upon her magic.

The shadows inside her stirred, still restless, but they answered her call.

Slowly, Nicola raised her hand, and the shadows coiled around her fingers, solid and strong.

"I am not yours," she said, her voice steady now. "The shadows belong to me."

The figure's hand faltered, and for a moment, the air around it shimmered, as though it was losing its shape. The academy was testing her, pushing her, but she had to be stronger now. She *could* have control. She wasn't the same person she was when she arrived at Darkmore Academy, lost and confused.

She was different now.

With a sharp flick of her wrist, Nicola sent shadows surging forward. They crashed into the figure. The force of her magic pushed the illusion to shatter, the writhing walls around her dissolving into nothingness. The figure disappeared, its very essence fading into the void as the room shifted once more.

When the shadows cleared, Nicola found

herself standing in the centre of her room again. The walls were solid, the door was real, and the suffocating presence of the academy had lessened.

But it wasn't over.

She could still feel it – watching, waiting, assessing her. The academy wasn't finished with her yet, and it wouldn't be satisfied until she had truly proven herself.

She collapsed onto the edge of her bed, the adrenaline from the encounter still coursing through her veins. The shadows inside her had quietened, but she knew they were still there, waiting for her next command.

She could have sworn the academy had been attempting to break her, to push her past the limits of sanity. But she had survived. And she had won.

For now.

Chapter Twelve

The calm over the next few days was fleeting. Nicola could constantly feel a presence lurking in the background, always just out of sight but never truly gone. Whatever it was that was trying to test her, she knew it would only be a matter of time before it struck again.

Each day, she felt something pushing, testing her limits, waiting for her to break. The shadows within her were subdued, but never silent. They whispered to her in the night, urging her to give in to them, to let them consume her entirely. Fortunately, she still had enough of herself left to resist, and she clung to that sliver of control like a lifeline.

Late one evening, as the academy's curfew bell rang out across the grounds, Nicola found herself in the empty courtyard, pacing beneath the looming height of the old tower. The moon was hidden behind a thick layer of clouds, casting the world in a dim, silvery light. The fog that always surrounded the academy clung to the ground in thick swirls, wrapping around her feet as she walked.

The shadows were restless tonight. She could feel them in the air, in the stone walls of the academy. The entire place seemed to be holding its breath, waiting for something.

As she stared up at the old tower, there was something about it that called to her. The shadows inside her stirred, and before she knew it, her feet were carrying her to the building's entrance.

The door was still slightly ajar, just as it had been the night she found the mirror. She hesitated at the threshold, but the shadows inside her pushed her forward, urging her to enter.

She stepped inside the tower to be met with silence. As she ventured further, the air remained thick with the scent of dust and decay, as though it hadn't been disrupted. The same narrow spiral staircase stretched up into the darkness. The faint glow of moonlight filtered in through the murky windows, casting long shadows across the floor. Everything was exactly as she remembered it, but the energy in every part, every crevice, had changed.

On edge, but now following an overwhelming sense of instinct, Nicola made her way up the staircase, the soles of her shoes soft against the crumbling stone steps. The shadows swirled around her, faster now. The very atmosphere seemed to throb with a dark energy, an undercurrent of something threatening and hostile. It wasn't the kind of magic that invited exploration – it demanded caution, as though warning her that this place wasn't meant for trespassers. Yet it also pulled her forward, as if daring her to climb higher, to see what lay hidden at the top.

When she reached the top, the circular room at the peak of the tower was just as she had left it. The faded tapestries still hung on the walls, and the thick layer of dust still covered the floor. But the pedestal in the centre of the room was different.

The black mirror was no longer there.

Instead, a figure – tall and cloaked in shadows – stood facing away from Nicola, but as though they had been waiting for her. The figure's head was hidden beneath a black hood, its body wrapped in tendrils of shadow that flickered and twisted like smoke. The air around it crackled with power, old and dangerous, and Nicola could feel the academy's magic pulsing through it, like the heartbeat of the building itself.

Her breath caught in her throat as the figure turned to face her, its eyes – devoid of discernable pupils – glowing an eerie red in the dim light. This figure wasn't just an illusion. This was something real. Something tangible.

"The academy has been watching you," the figure said, its voice low and deep. "It knows what you are."

"Stop this," Nicola said, tired of having to play this game. "I don't belong to the academy."

The figure's eyes narrowed, and for a moment, the shadows around it seemed to darken.

"You are wrong," they said. "The shadows inside you are part of this place. You are bound to it."

Nicola shook her head, trying to push back the rising panic.

"I control the shadows," she said, not fully convinced of her own words. "They don't control me."

The figure took a step closer, its sable robes brushing against the floor.

"You are mistaken," they said firmly. "The shadows have always been part of the academy's power. You have simply borrowed them. But now, the academy demands more."

"I... but... That ritual... I thought... That mirror... I didn't mean to..."

"You don't have to give in," the figure interrupted, its voice softer now, almost coaxing. "You can still break free. But truly, it will come at a cost."

"What cost?" Nicola asked anxiously, suspiciously.

The figure didn't answer right away. Instead, it reached out a hand, its fingers long and thin, gnarled like the branches of a dead tree. The shadows in the room seemed to pulse in time with the movement, and for a moment, Nicola felt the full weight of the academy's presence pressing down on her.

"If you wish to free yourself from the academy, you must sever the connection completely," the figure said, its voice steady and calm. "But doing so will cost you your magic. The shadows will no longer be with you, and they certainly won't answer to you. You will be ordinary – just another student without power."

Nicola felt sick. The thought of losing her magic entirely was terrifying. She had lived her whole life feeling like an outcast, disconnected from everyone else because of her power. But without it, who would she be?

However, the alternative was surely worse. If she stayed bound to the academy, if she let the shadows consume her, she would lose herself completely. She would have no control over her magic. The ongoing battle could be soul-destroying in the end – to the point of insanity.

The figure's eyes gleamed, as though it could sense Nicola's inner turmoil.

"The choice is yours," they said. "Remain bound to the shadows and the academy, or give up your power in the knowledge that it will grant you your freedom."

For a moment, Nicola struggled to breathe. Her thoughts churned. This wasn't something to be taken lightly. There was so much at stake that every other decision she'd made in her life felt so small in comparison to this. This wasn't just a choice; it was *the* choice, the kind that could alter everything, and there would be no turning back once it was made.

It angered her that the academy was testing her like this; evidently, it wanted to see if she would give in. A part of her felt that she'd fought too hard to let this place take everything from her.

But then, she took a deep breath, conscious that she needed to steady herself. As much as magic had always been a part of her, coursing through her veins since the day she was born, it had never brought her peace. It was the reason she had been rejected from every other school, the very reason she had been sent here – to Darkmore Academy. Her magic, so wild and unpredictable, had haunted her every step, warping her life into something she barely recognised. The thought of freedom, of no longer having to deal with the relentless surge of power, was intoxicating. What would it be like to wake up and not feel the shadows pulling her in every direction? To simply be, without fear, demands or chaos always at her heels? She longed for that, for a life where magic didn't dictate her every move. The thought still terrified her, purely because it was so different from anything she had ever known, but it also offered a glimpse of the peace she had been yearning for, long before this place had become part of the equation.

She met the figure's glowing red eyes, feeling a surge of defiance and relief.

"I don't want this anymore," she said, her voice steady, though the enormity of the decision pressed against her. "Take my magic. All of it. I want to be free."

The figure's lips curled into something that

wasn't quite a smile but looked like satisfaction.

"Are you sure?" they said, surprising Nicola with their question. "Once your magic is gone, it cannot be returned. No second chances."

"I'm sure," Nicola replied firmly. "My powers have caused me a lot of trouble in the past. Every day, I wake with the uncertainty of how they're going to respond to the world around me... There is clearly a reason why I've been sent here. Whether it's destiny or merely the right opportunity at the right time, I feel that I'd be foolish not to embrace it."

"Very well," said the figure, its voice no longer carrying the edge of menace Nicola had initially felt.

Now, as the figure moved closer, it felt more like a companion, a kindred spirit, perhaps – an entity not here to harm, but to guide. The glowing red eyes, once sharp and threatening, now seemed to watch Nicola with an almost solemn understanding. The being moved with purpose, but without malice, like a shadow that had always been there, waiting patiently for this moment to help Nicola shed the burden she no longer wished to carry.

Suddenly and decisively, the figure raised its hand and flicked an invisible spot in the air with its long, bony fingers. The walls of the tower groaned, and the very stones beneath Nicola's feet began to tremble. Shadows, thicker and darker than ever before, coiled around her, drawn from every part of the room. The atmosphere became rich with magic, suffocating and exhilarating all at once.

The figure raised its other hand and began muttering in a language Nicola had never heard. The words seemed to tear at the fabric of reality itself, and the tower felt as though it had been transported to some otherworldly realm. Everything swirled and then went black as tendrils of obsidian spun faster around them, wrapping around Nicola's body and prying into her very soul.

She gasped as the shadows reached inside her and began to pull. It felt like something vital was being ripped away, an unbearable weight being lifted from her chest. Her magic

– that wild, untamed force that had been with her since birth – started to pour out of her in torrents to be sucked into the figure's outstretched hands like ink drawn from a well. The sensation was both painful and liberating – her veins felt empty, her body lighter. She was losing her magic, but with it, she was shedding the burden she had carried for so long.

The figure chanted louder, its voice growing deeper, resonating with ancient authority. It threw its head back, absorbing the torrent of magic with an almost feverish hunger. Dark energy crackled through the air as Nicola felt the last remnants of her power slipping away.

Then, with a final word, the figure clenched its fists, and the shadows exploded outwards, dissolving into nothingness. The ritual was over.

Nicola collapsed to the floor, gasping for breath, her body trembling. She felt so different, lighter than ever before.

When she looked up, the figure was gone. The tower was silent, save for her ragged breathing echoing in the stillness. She was alone, utterly and completely. The room, now devoid of the ominous presence it had once held, felt empty and strangely peaceful.

Exhaustion gripped her, but so did exhilaration. She stood slowly, her limbs heavy but unburdened. The air felt different, cleaner. She inhaled deeply, closing her eyes for a moment.

She was no longer the scared young woman who had come to Darkmore Academy haunted by uncontrollable magic.

It was truly over. For the first time in her life, she felt free. Free from the shadows, and free from the magic that had defined her every action and thought.

Chapter Thirteen

The night was still and silent as Nicola stepped out of the tower. For so long, the shadows had been a part of her, defining her, making her feel powerful even when they had threatened to overwhelm her. Now, without them, she felt exposed, vulnerable, like a piece of her was no longer there.

Despite the strangeness of this new sensation, however, this was what she had chosen. She had broken free from the academy's grasp, from the ancient magic that had tried to consume her. She had won.

The cold air bit at her skin as she crossed the courtyard, barely aware of her surroundings, her thoughts distant. She was just another student now – just another face in the crowd. No longer dangerous, no longer different. Ordinary.

And, despite the newness of that feeling, despite what she had feared, it didn't feel too bad at all.

As Nicola made her way along the hallways towards her dorm room, the academy no longer felt foreboding. There was nothing around her, or in the walls, that called to her or caught her attention out of the corner of her vision. There was no weight pressing down on her, no lingering sense of an unwelcome presence that required her vigilance.

"Hey."

The voice took Nicola from her reverie, but it didn't startle her. It was Remy, approaching from one of the corridors, her eyes scanning Nicola's face as if searching for answers.

"Are you alright?" Remy asked, though the anticipation in her tone suggested she already knew the answer.

"I'm free," Nicola blurted, certain that Remy would understand.

Remy's gaze flickered with something like

relief, but there was also a hint of sadness there.

"You broke the bond?"

"Yes," Nicola said straight away. "The academy can't demand anything of me anymore."

There was a long pause. Remy's eyes softened as she stepped closer, her expression one of concern.

"You paid the price, didn't you?"

It wasn't really a question. Nicola was certain that Remy knew, and always had.

"I don't have the shadows anymore," Nicola said quietly. "There's not a single ounce of magic in me now. I'm just... normal."

"Maybe that's not such a bad thing," Remy said gently, with empathy and understanding. "The shadows... they were dangerous. They tried to consume you, but now you're free. You're still you, with or without magic."

There was something about Remy's words that gave Nicola a pleasant feeling of calm. She had spent so long defining herself by her magic, by the shadows that had set her apart, that she hadn't stopped to think about who she was without them. She had always feared being ordinary, being powerless, but perhaps Remy was right. Maybe being free from the shadows didn't mean she was less than before – it just meant she was different now.

"I guess I just don't know who I am without them," Nicola admitted.

"You're still you," Remy said kindly. "You've always been you. Your powers didn't define that."

"Thank you," said Nicola, feeling a new flicker of hope.

"Anyway," Remy said companionably, "I'd better turn in, and so should you. Now that you don't have to worry about the shadows anymore, you should make sure none of the professors catch you breaking curfew!"

With that, Remy turned and headed off down the corridor, her footsteps light and purposeful.

Nicola took a deep breath, savouring the calm that enveloped her. The lingering tension from earlier felt like a distant memory as she walked towards her room, each step a reminder that the shadows no longer had power over her.

The familiar creak of her door felt reassuring as she pushed it open, and for the first time, her room felt warm and inviting. No longer was it somewhere to suffer unpleasant visions in place of a good night's sleep.

As Nicola settled into the newfound comfort of her room, a sudden realisation gripped her: the forbidden book was still tucked away in her desk drawer. Perhaps now that she was without magic, the presence of the book wouldn't feel as unsettling, but she couldn't be sure. The thought of seeing it again was still unnerving after everything that had happened.

She hesitated for a moment. Then, with a deep breath to steady her nerves, she cautiously opened the drawer, bracing herself for whatever darkness might greet her.

To her surprise, instead of the ominous tome, she found a handwritten note. Frowning in curiosity, she plucked it out and unfolded the paper. She smiled to herself as she recognised Remy's handwriting scrawled across the page.

Dear Nicola,

Don't worry about the book. I have taken care of it for you and returned it to the library. You won't have to see it again.

Remy

The words filled Nicola with an unexpected sense of relief and gratitude. It was a simple gesture, but it showed her that she had a friend who cared. Since meeting Remy from the boat that fateful day, there had been moments where Nicola had found Remy's intensity to be eerie – her piercing gaze, the way she seemed to know things about people without them saying a word, and the uncanny way she navigated her way around the academy. Now though, Nicola could see how deeply invested Remy was in looking out for her, how fiercely she had sought to defend her against the darker aspects of this place.

Nicola yawned and contentedly stretched her arms. She kicked off her shoes and changed into comfortable clothes, then fluffed her pillow. As she eased her way into bed, pulling the soft covers up to her chin, she embraced the sense of peace, grateful for the chance to finally rest.

Chapter Fourteen

The following days were surreal. Nicola moved through her classes with a sense of detachment, no longer burdened by the constant pull of the shadows. The whispers that had once filled her mind were gone, and had been replaced by a quiet that felt both unfamiliar and liberating. Without the shadows, she had expected to feel weaker, but instead, she found herself noticing things she hadn't before.

The magic she had struggled with for so long had been chaotic, constantly pulling her in different directions. Now, without it, she felt grounded. Present. She could focus on her studies without the constant distraction of the darkness gnawing at the edges of her mind.

It was a strange kind of freedom – one she hadn't expected to find in the absence of power.

Remy stuck close, never letting Nicola drift too far into her own thoughts. Their camaraderie was such that now, the academy felt less like a place of isolation and more like something Nicola could navigate, something she could handle.

Occasionally, Nicola would catch herself wondering about the shadows, instinctively preparing to call upon the magic that had once been a part of her, only to remember that it was no longer there. Each time, she reminded herself that it had been her choice. Yes, she had sacrificed a major part of herself, but in having done so, she had broken free.

As the days passed, the lack of magic started to feel normal to Nicola, rather than new and unusual.

She wasn't the same person she had been when she arrived at Darkmore Academy. She had grown, changed. The shadows no longer had a hold on her, and for the first time, she felt like she could breathe.

One evening, as she and Remy sat outside by the courtyard, watching the fog roll in over the grounds, Nicola realised something she hadn't thought possible.

She was happy.

Maybe not in the way she had once imagined – powerful and in control of her magic – but in a different way. She was happy because she had made it through. She had survived, and though she had lost a part of herself along the way, she had found something else. Something better.

She glanced over at Remy, who was staring off into the distance, her expression thoughtful.

"Thank you," Nicola said softly.

Remy raised an eyebrow, turning to face her.

"For what?"

"For sticking by me," Nicola replied sincerely. "For helping me find myself."

Remy smiled a warm, genuine smile that lit up her face.

"You're more than welcome," she said. "One less soul lost to the darkness means everything to me. Besides, as soon as I laid eyes on you, I sensed that you'd be a good friend."

As the fog settled, wrapping the academy in its familiar embrace, Nicola realised that maybe, just maybe, she had finally found her place in the world – free from the shadows, but stronger than ever.

www.ingramcontent.com/pod-product-compliance
Lightning Source LLC
Chambersburg PA
CBHW031004210726
48290CB00007B/2470